DogFish

For my darling son, Gabriel,
king of the hypnotising eyes...
I LOVE YOU – **GS**

For Mum, Dad,
Lee, Claire and Andrew – **DT**

SIMON AND SCHUSTER
First published in Great Britain in 2008
by Simon and Schuster UK Ltd
Africa House, 64-78 Kingsway, London, WC2B 6AH
A CBS Company

Text copyright © 2008 Gillian Shields
Illustrations © 2008 Dan Taylor

The right of Gillian Shields and Dan Taylor to be
identified as the author and illustrator of this work
has been asserted by them in accordance with the
Copyright, Designs and Patents Act, 1988

A CIP catalogue record for this book is available
from the British Library upon request

ISBN: 978 1 41691 042 8 (HB)
ISBN: 978 1 41691 043 5 (PB)

Printed in Singapore

1 3 5 7 9 10 8 6 4 2

DogFish

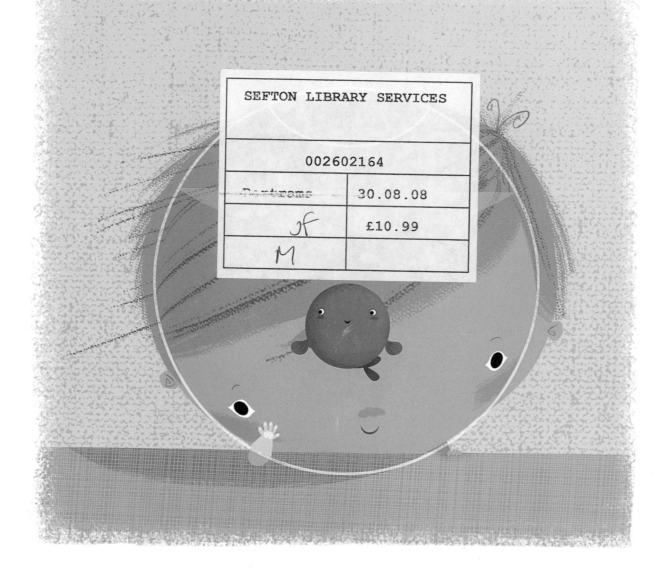

Gillian Shields

Illustrated by Dan Taylor

SIMON AND SCHUSTER
London · New York · Sydney

Everyone has a dog . . .

except me.

So I say to my mum,
"I need a dog."

But my mum says,
    "Why do you need a dog when
    you have such a nice goldfish?"

She always says things like that.

I explain that goldfish cannot . . .

catch sticks,

or go for walks,

or sit by your feet.

And they NEVER
wag their tails.

"That is why," I say, looking at her with my hypnotising eyes,

"I NEED A DOG."

But my mum says,
  "We'll see," which really means, "**NO**."

I look sad.
  My goldfish looks sad too.

These are our sad looks.

So my mum says, in her kind-and-caring voice,
   "But, honey, how could we have a dog
   when we live on the forty-fourth floor?"

I think for a bit and say,
"Four hundred and forty-four
stairs would be very good
exercise for a dog."

Then she says, in her soothing-and-explaining voice,
"But, sweetheart, wouldn't the dog be bored
all day, when I'm at work and you're in school?"

So I think a bit more and say,
"It could read the paper?"

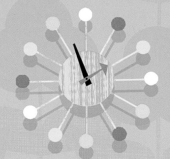

And my mum looks irritated
but sorrowful. Like this.

Then she says, in her this-really-is-the-end-
of-the-matter voice,
"Now, darling, how could we possibly
afford to feed a great big hungry dog?"

But I say, as quick as a fish,
"I don't want a big hungry dog. I want
a very, very, very small dog that eats
hardly anything at all. Just scraps."

Then we all look how people look when
The Situation is Hopeless. Like this.

After a bit, my mum says,
     "Well, if you can't have what you want,
     you could try to want what you have."

She ALWAYS says things like that.

So then I look at my goldfish.

And my goldfish looks at me
with his hypnotising eyes, and I think,

"Maybe . . . just maybe . . ."

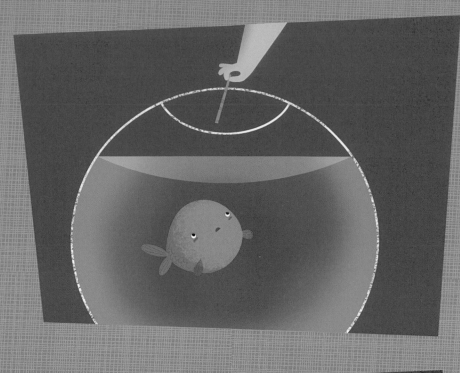

So I teach my goldfish
to catch a teeny
tiny stick.

It takes practice.

It is a tough job.

Sometimes I think it is
A Waste of
Time.

But we get there in the end – and it feels good!

This is how good it feels.

I take my goldfish for walks . . .

. . .and he takes me for walks.

We climb
the four hundred
and forty-four stairs –

together.

When we are out, he reads the paper.
He's never bored.

He

eats

hardly

anything

at all.

Just scraps.

In the evening, he sits by my feet,
and I tell him stuff. He's a great listener.

He can even wag his tail to say, "I love you."
He's not just a goldfish . . .

He's a DOGfish!

So now, when I see everyone with
their ordinary old dogs, I say . . .

"Why would I need a dog when I
have the best goldfish in the world?"

I like saying that.

And I look, and my mum looks, and my
goldfish looks utterly, totally, blissfully…

HAPPY!

Just like this.

THE END